THE COSTUME PARTY

AN EROTIC ADVENTURE

VICTORIA RUSH

VOLUME 16

JADE'S EROTIC ADVENTURES - BOOK 16

COPYRIGHT

The Costume Party © 2019 Victoria Rush

Cover Design © 2019 PhotoMaras

Everybody's an exhibitionist in disguise...

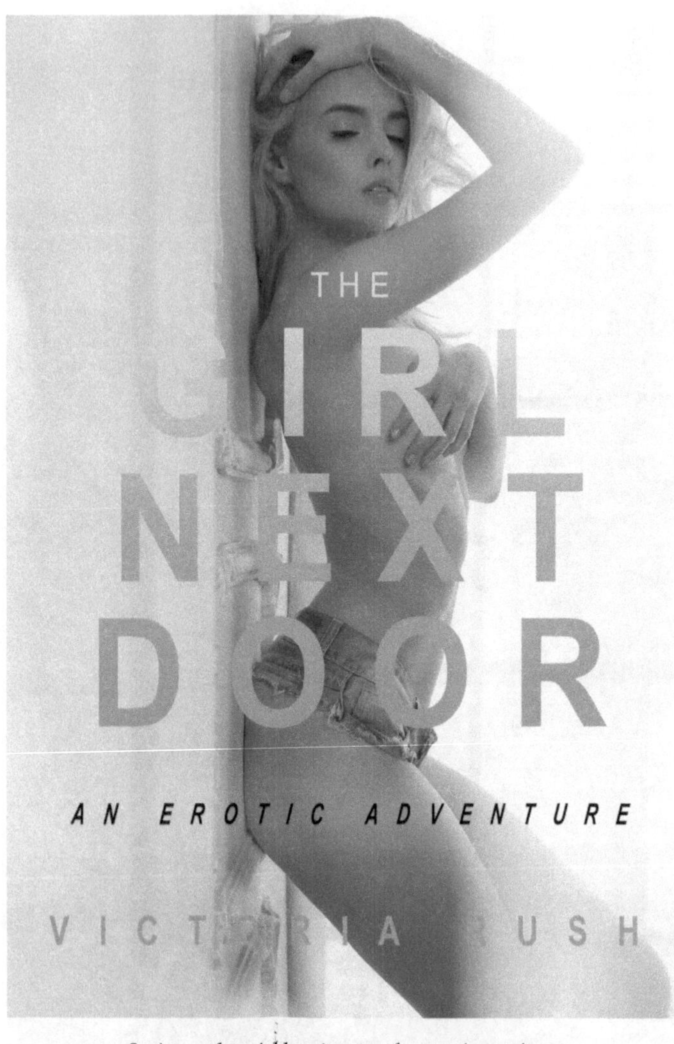

Spying on the neighbors just got a lot more interesting...

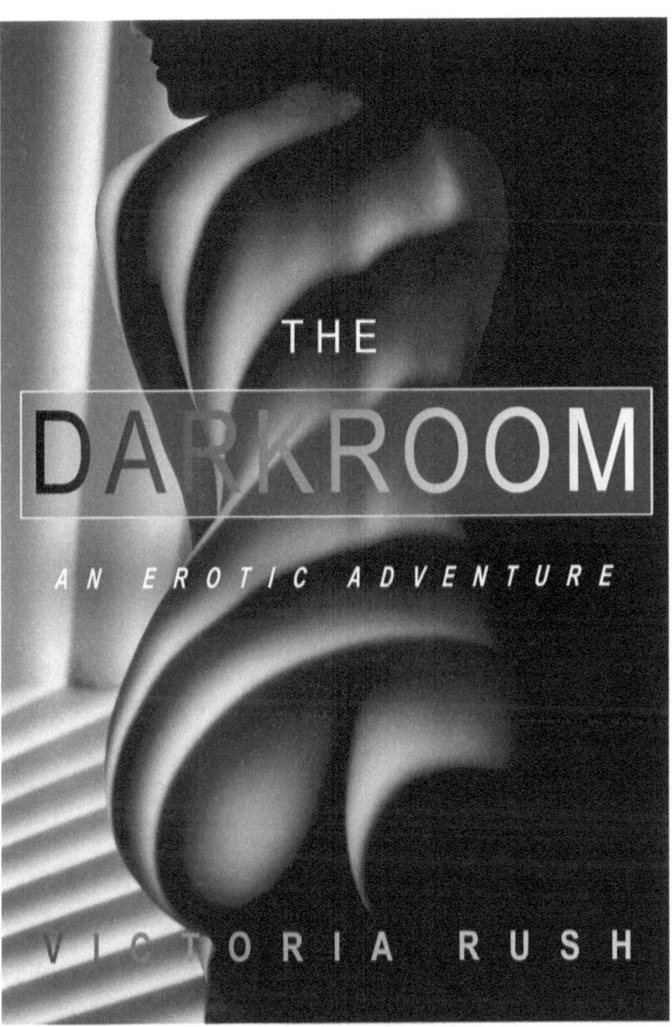

Everything's sexier in the dark...

Artificial intelligence never felt so real...

Books 6 - 10 in the bestselling series - now 60% off.

For the uninhibited...

1

───────

I woke up to the sound of my best friend Hannah calling me from the other end of my house. She'd let herself in early on a Saturday morning and for some reason was yelling at me as she ran up the stairs.

"Jade!" she hollered. "Where are you? I've got some exciting news!"

I rolled over and squinted at my clock on the nightstand. It was a little past eight. Saturdays were the only day of the week I allowed myself to sleep in, and I was more than a little ticked at her rude intrusion.

"Aren't you up yet?" she called. "Get up—you're not going to believe what I just heard."

I rolled over and wrapped my pillow around my ears as she dashed into my bedroom. She paused for a minute smiling at my feeble attempt to block her out of my morning daze, then she pounced on the bed below my curled-up knees.

"Wake up, sleepyhead!" she squealed, pushing my shoulders to rouse me from my slumber.

"This better be good," I said, raising my pillow a few

inches and peering at her through thin eyes. "You know how much I worship my weekend sleep-ins."

"You'll be glad I woke you when you hear what I have to tell you," she said. "Besides, you're gonna want to get up and begin planning your day right away. We're going to need a few extra hours to go shopping."

I pulled my duvet cover over my shoulders and huffed.

"What could possibly be so important to drag me out of my soft and cozy bed this early in the morning?"

I peered outside, looking at the gray clouds hanging low in the late October skies. I was in no hurry to venture out into the chilly autumn air.

"Only the biggest private shindig of the year. Steve Bannon is hosting his annual Halloween party at his mansion on the lake, and we're invited!"

"Isn't that the party with all the A-list celebrities? How did you score an invitation?"

Hannah peered at me with a wicked look in her eyes.

"Let's just say I know somebody who knows somebody. Someone with whom I may have pulled a few strings to earn some special favors."

"I bet that's not the *only* thing you were pulling to earn those favors," I said, raising an eyebrow.

"Possibly," she smirked. "But I apparently impressed him enough with my naked gymnastics to land an invitation to this special event. Except this year, it's got an extra twist. This time it's going to be a *nude* costume party."

I lifted my head and propped the side of my face on a crooked elbow, suddenly intrigued.

"Isn't that an oxymoron? How can you be in costume and naked at the same time?"

Hannah smiled and handed me a gold-embossed card inscribed with fancy calligraphy writing. I felt the raised surface of the script on the tips of fingers, rubbing it gently trying to divine its meaning through my still bleary eyes. Somebody had gone to a great deal of effort to create an invitation card on par with the most extravagant wedding.

I pulled myself up and leaned against my headboard, slowly reading the message.

You are cordially invited to attend my annual Halloween costume ball at my estate overlooking Lake Michigan.

This year I've added a special twist to make it even more interesting. You're encouraged to wear as little or as much trappings as you feel comfortable—including nothing at all beyond a simple mask. With everyone baring a little more than usual, who knows what kind of shenanigans might break out, and we're always mindful of protecting the anonymity of our special guests.

Of course, I encourage everyone to be playful and creative with their choice of costumes, as this is always the highlight of the event. As in previous years, there will be a special prize for the best costume of the evening and we hope you'll be suitably daring and inventive.

Feel free to bring a partner and let down your britches! As always, what happens at the Bannon residence stays at the Bannon residence. I look forward to seeing you this Saturday, starting at midnight. We'll all have a ghoulish good time!

I peered up at Hannah and grinned.

"No RSVP?"

"There's no need with a Steve Bannon invitation," she said. Everyone who's invited always goes. It's the go-to event of the year in the Chicago area. Models, actresses, rock stars, billionaires—everybody who's anybody in this town will be there. There's even a rumor that the Governor and his wife will attend this year's event."

I looked down at the card, rubbing my fingers over the embossed script.

"The invitation says you're allowed to bring a partner. Was that a condition of your little tryst with your friend—that you accompany him as his plus-one?"

Hannah peered at me devilishly as a tiny curl formed on the sides of her mouth.

"When I told him I had a friend who was even prettier than me and had a body to die for, he didn't hesitate to hand me an extra invitation. *You're* my plus-one, girl." She pulled another card out of her purse and handed it to me. "You know I'd never pass up an opportunity like this without bringing my bestie along to share in the fun."

I looked at Hannah with a quizzical look and shook my head in confusion.

"How are we ever going to find a decent Halloween costume on the Saturday before the end of the month? All the costume stores will be sold out of the best stuff."

Hannah kicked off her shoes and lifted the covers, then scooched in excitedly next to me against the headboard.

"I've been searching online for some ideas. We don't have to wear anything too elaborate, and there's no reason why we have to stick to a Halloween theme. Remember, this is a *nude* costume party. We already look pretty hot for a couple of girls nearing middle age. The less we wear, the better. Let's flaunt it while we've still got it!"

She pulled an iPad out of her purse and tapped the screen. A website opened showing a collection of sexy models wearing risqué costumes. She scrolled through the images, commenting on the various themes.

"Just look at some of these possibilities. We can play

any role we like, wearing as much or as little as we please. Most of these costumes can be put together with a simple trip to Walmart and maybe a bit of needle and thread. Plus, we can easily remove one of two pieces from each outfit to reveal a bit more skin. The most important element is the headpiece. We just need something to conceal our identity and highlight our girly figures with a bit of flair."

Hannah paused at a picture of a sexy blonde wearing a Playboy bunny costume. She wore a tight corset and a rubber mask that covered the top half of her face with tall ears pointing up in the air.

"What about this one? You have to admit, it's pretty hot. You'd could even dispense with the bodice altogether and just keep the bunny tail on your naked ass. Imagine the looks you'd get prancing around his mansion in that costume!"

The images of sexy half-nude models wearing unusual masks reminded me of my encounter at the Fantasy Feast naked dinner party. Suddenly, I became mindful of the wetness that had begun building between my legs.

"Not bad," I said, shifting my weight uncomfortably off the wet spot on my sheets. "Show me some more."

Hannah flipped through a few more images and stopped at a picture of a sexy maid wearing a lacy dress, holding a feather duster in her hand. Her firm tits pressed against the flimsy fabric, creating an irresistible focal point from the sensuous shadows on her bosom.

"How about this?" she said. "You'd look stunning in this outfit. You'd be covering up just enough to drive every man and woman at that party absolutely crazy. And imagine all the fun you could have teasing the naked guests with your little duster!"

"Intriguing..." I said as I squeezed my thighs together, trying to quiet my burning clit.

The more images Hannah showed me, the more turned on I got. Whether it was from me imagining myself in the costumes or imagining myself playing with the guests dressed up in the provocative outfits, was unclear. Either way, the more my mind began to ponder the possibilities, the more excited I became about going to this event.

"The only problem is, it will be difficult to cover my face without looking unnatural in that outfit," I frowned. "Show me more costumes with masks."

Hannah refined her search by typing in the words *sexy mask costumes* and the screen refreshed showing a new set of models in racy outfits. Many of the themes revolved around superheroes, with the male models sporting Batman and Superman motifs and the female models wearing Wonder Woman and Batgirl-type costumes.

"Not very original," I frowned. "I bet there'll be a ton of superhero costumes among all those egotistical celebrities. I'm looking for something a little different."

Hannah paused for a moment, then tapped on her photo library pulling up an image of me wearing a business suit painted on my naked body.

"Remember that time you went to the nude body-painting workshop? You're a graphic artist. You can be virtually anything you want and show off all you wish with a little bit of well-disguised paint. Whether it's Catwoman, Black Widow, or Wonder Woman—all these characters wear is a mask and tight outfits to show off their beautiful physiques. You could even dress up like Mystique in the X-Men movie and wear absolutely nothing other than a full coat of body paint."

"Been there, done that," I said. "If I'm going to really

enjoy myself, I want to wear something I've never worn before that will absolutely blow everyone away."

"You sure are a tough customer," Hannah said, shaking her head. "Let's try something a little different..."

She reopened her browser and typed in the words *naked masquerade costumes*. A gallery of Google images popped up with a collection of half-naked men and women.

"*Now* we're talking," I said, squirming on the bed as I scanned the toned bodies of the sexy models.

"Look at that one," Hannah said, pointing at the screen. "It's a picture of Rihanna at last year's Met Gala dressed as Nefertiti. With her sheer lace dress and silver headdress, it doesn't leave much to the imagination. A bit more makeup around the eyes, and you'd be able to mask your identity quite easily."

"That's pretty hot," I said, beginning to feel the sheets getting wetter and wetter between my legs. "She definitely looks fuckable. But it's been done before. I don't want to wear something half of these people will have already seen."

"Damn, girl, you're *impossible!* Remember, less is more. The idea is to show as much of our bodies as possible to attract the attention of all these beautiful people. You could get away with a simple mask, a painted emblem on your chest, and a shiny belt. Who really cares what you're wearing as long as you get the attention of the guests?"

"Humor me for a little longer," I said, squeezing Hannah's leg. "I'm starting to get a few ideas. I just need a bit more inspiration."

Hannah began flipping through the images more quickly until one picture suddenly caught my attention.

"Wait!" I said. "Go back a few frames. I saw something interesting..."

She scrolled back until an image of six men dressed in contrasting costumes popped up.

"That's the one," I said, scanning the image slowly.

"*The Village People*?" Hannah said. "That might be okay for a gay guy, but how could you possibly look sexy wearing any one of those cheesy costumes?"

My eyes darted back and forth between the sexy cowboy wearing chaps and the indian warrior wearing a feathered headdress and a skimpy loincloth. Suddenly I nodded as a mischievous smile formed on my face.

"What?" Hannah said. "What could you possibly be thinking?"

She glanced down at my breasts peeking above the covers, noticing my hardening nipples.

"Because I know gay dudes—even ones with hard bodies like these guys—don't do it for you. Where is your mind going with this idea?"

"I've decided what I'm going to wear," I said, crossing my arms over my chest. "But I'm going to keep it a secret until we get to the party. It'll be all the more fun and surprising if I reveal it at the last second. But I promise you, it'll be one-of-a-kind and extremely provocative."

Hannah's eyes darted across my face, trying to imagine what I had in mind.

"Now you've got *me* all excited thinking what you're going to do. Judging by your obvious state of arousal, your head is already at the party. Can I crawl under the covers with you and have some fun fantasizing which one of those costumes you're going to wear?"

"By all means," I said, disappearing under the covers with her. "Just imagine me as one of those hot dudes with his clothes off."

"Mmm," Hannah purred, slithering between my slippery

thighs. "I'd rather imagine you as a hot *chick* with her clothes off."

"In a couple of days," I said, spreading my legs further apart and pulling her face into my steaming crotch. "You might be able to have it both ways."

2

Just after midnight on the day of the party, I pulled my car up beside a call box in front of a large wrought-iron gate protecting the entrance to Steve Bannon's estate. After providing our names and the identification numbers on the front of our invitation cards, the gates opened and we followed the curved driveway up to the front of a giant French-styled chateau. As a parking attendant approached our car, I turned to Hannah seated next to me and smiled.

"It's show time," I said.

"Not a moment too soon," she huffed. "I've been dying to see what you're wearing under that coat ever since you picked me up."

I'd intentionally worn a long western duster to cover my body all the way from my shoulders to my ankles. Part of it was meant to surprise Hannah when I finally reached the event, but it had much more to do with my desire to shock everyone else once I got in the front door. I reached behind my seat and pulled a thin black mask out of a bag on the floor and wrapped it around the top of my face.

Hannah's forehead wrinkled as she looked at me, still confused.

"Let me guess: Kato, Zorro, Nightshade?"

"You're moving in the right direction with the first two," I smiled, reaching back into the bag and pulling out a pair of western boots.

"Cowboy boots?" Hannah squinted. "I don't know my cowboy characters quite as well—"

"Maybe this will help," I said, donning a white Stetson.

Hannah looked at me blankly for a moment, then her eyes lit up, recognizing the familiar image of the famous cowboy with the white hat and black mask.

"The Lone Ranger?"

"Yes, but with a little twist. You'll have to wait for the full reveal until we get inside."

"You're such a tease," she said as I handed the attendant my keys and we stepped out of the car.

We paused for a moment, taking in the full scale of the Bannon estate close-up. The four-story mansion extended almost a hundred feet in either direction, with tall arched windows and ornate brickwork. The bright spotlights illuminating the front of the house lit up the entire courtyard, reflecting off Hannah's shiny Batgirl outfit.

"Holy shit!" she exclaimed. "This place is gigantic. We're going to have to drop *breadcrumbs* to not get lost in there."

"More like *caviar* or *foie gras*," I chuckled. "Something tells me everything about this affair is going to be top shelf."

"What are we waiting for?" Hannah giggled, rushing ahead of me toward the front door.

My gaze drifted down while I soaked up her tight ass in her black latex outfit. She had a beautiful hourglass figure, and the tight Batgirl costume highlighted every curve of her sexy body. I smiled as I imagined the two of us mingling among the high rollers. But I had a feeling they'd be focused on someone *else's* ass tonight.

With the large double entrance doors pulled back, we peered into the bright marble-floored foyer as we approached the front steps. A large crowd of costumed guests had already begun to gather in the main ballroom, and we could hear soft jazz music wafting out into the courtyard.

"Good evening ladies," a man wearing a crisply tailored tailcoat and black tie said as we stepped into the entrance hall.

He looked at my long shawl and smiled.

"May I check your coat, Madam?"

"Yes, thank you," I said, turning my back to assist him in its removal.

When he pulled the cape off my back and viewed my naked backside, I heard him gasp. To complement my Lone Ranger disguise, I'd chosen to wear a tight-fitting black leather vest and long black chaps with nothing underneath. My tight ass poked out the back of the open leggings, and I could feel him running his eyes up and down my body as he hesitated hanging my coat in the closet.

But when I turned around, both Hannah and the doorman took a step back in shock. On the front of my open pants, I wore a large dildo fashioned in the shape of a man's cock and balls, framed by two silver pistols on either side of my hips. The long phallus slapped against the sides of my naked thighs as it swung from side to side.

"Holy *fuck*, Jade!" Hannah squealed. "That's *outrageous*! Where did you ever come up with that idea?"

"Remember the Village People picture you showed me a

few days ago? I decided to borrow elements of both the cowboy and the indian characters to create my own design." I shook my hips to juggle my equipment and smiled. "I thought it would be kind of fun playing *both* sides of coin, so to speak."

"Uh—*yeah*," she said, flicking her eyes between my tight bosom spilling over the top of my vest and my faux genitals. "I'd have to say you pulled it off. With that getup, I expect you'll be the center of attention all night long."

"Um," the doorman said, shyly interrupting. "May I have your tickets, please?"

"Of course," I said, rustling my rubber balls as I fished in the pocket of my chaps for my ticket. When the butler turned to collect Hannah's ticket, I could see the front of his pants tenting in obvious arousal.

"Enjoy your evening," he said, motioning for us to enter the ballroom.

"Oh, I have a feeling we will," Hannah winked, as she nodded toward the lengthening pole pushing down his pant leg.

A waiter approached us with tall glasses of champagne on a silver tray and did a double-take when he noticed the swinging package between my legs.

"Whoa boy," Hannah said to the server, taking two glasses off his unsteady tray. "We wouldn't want you to spill your load before we've sampled the goods."

As we moved into the main entrance hall, the patrons milling in small groups began to turn around to view the newly arriving guests. Suddenly, the gentle buzz of group conversation receded until the only sound we could hear was the hum of the background music. Everyone was so stunned taking in my outfit, they were literally dumbstruck with their mouths agape.

Many of the guests had chosen to wear predictable Halloween costumes with little bits of flesh showing here and there, but nobody was letting it all hang out quite as brazenly as I had. Amid the predictable sprinkling of ghosts and goblins, there was a profusion of superhero figures and Disney characters bedecked in various stages of undress. I shook my head at the lack of imagination of the high-powered group and began to wonder if the event was going to live up to Hannah's hyperbole.

"Damn, girl," she said. "It looks like you're going to be this evening's scene-stealer. You've already stopped the show. I don't know what everybody's thinking right now, but that thing looks so realistic, they must be wondering if you're a legit tranny wearing that impressive package."

I smiled a crooked grin, suddenly feeling self-conscious with all of the eyes in the room surveying my exposed body. Fortunately, a handsome couple dressed as Anthony and Cleopatra began to approach us, providing some distraction.

"Welcome to our little costume party," the man said, extending his hand to Hannah and me. "I'm Steve Bannon and this is my wife Genevieve. You'll have to excuse me, but I don't recognize either of you under your—*interesting* disguises."

I was taken aback by how handsome the eccentric billionaire looked close up. With his square jaw, dimpled cheeks and thick head of salt-and-pepper hair swept back in a dense poof, he looked like a slightly older version of the famous actor Patrick Dempsey. He wore a loose toga draped over his well-muscled chest, and I could see his pecs flexing as he shook my hand.

But I found his wife even more beguiling. Wearing a tight-fitting gold-lamé dress slitted at one side of her hips and a pretty beaded headdress, she looked like a deadringer for a young Elizabeth Taylor. As I ran my eyes shamelessly over her luscious figure, I felt a sudden dampness building under the weight of my latex balls pressing against my flaring clit.

"Jade," I introduced myself, not yet wanting to reveal my full identity.

"Hannah," my partner responded, politely shaking their hands.

"It appears that you two have already captured the attention of my guests," Bannon said, turning to appraise the congregation still gazing awkwardly in our direction. He extended his arm in the direction of the main hall and nodded. "Please, come in and mingle. There are so many fascinating people to meet. I'm sure we'll catch up with the two of you a little later this evening."

"I'll look forward to that," I said, smiling at Genevieve, lingering for a moment longer at her dazzling figure. She returned the gesture, widening her eyes as my member twitched while I held my palm over the handle of one of my six-shooters.

"Holy shit," Hannah said, as Bannon and his wife melted back into the crowd. "Did you see the way he was looking at you? He was practically *raping* you with his eyes. Something tells me this is going to be a very interesting night. It seems the men are even more enamored with your disguise than the women. Either there's a lot of bi-curious guys in here, or they're attracted to that whole futa thing."

"I dunno," I said. "I'm showing off a lot of *girl* parts too. Who's to say what they're more attracted to? But did you notice his wife? I'd far rather get into *her* pants."

"It's too bad that thing isn't animated," Hannah chuckled, glancing at my pendulous dick. "If you could actually get it up, you could probably have your way with just about everybody in this place."

"Who knows?" I said, winking at Hannah. "In my current state of arousal, I wouldn't be surprised if this thing had a life of its own."

Little did she know how much truth in this statement I was about to reveal before the evening was over.

3

———

After Bannon and his wife resumed mingling with the rest of the crowd, Hannah and I wandered into the main ballroom. At first, most of the assembled groups gave us a wide berth, unsure what to make of the two girls dressed in such revealing costumes. Hannah's latex Batgirl outfit clung to her naked body like a second skin, the shiny fabric accentuating every crease and curve like it was painted on her. And the cutouts on both sides of my leather chaps left little to the imagination, even with the modicum of cover provided by my fake genitals covering my bare mound.

I was glad to have the freedom to mill about the room for a while, surveying the faces and costumes of the high-powered gathering. I recognized a fair number of public figures from the senior ranks of the local political, business, and media fields. The mayor was there with his wife, dressed as Little Red Riding Hood and the Big Bad Wolf, which seemed fitting given the ongoing level of corruption at City Hall. Bannon's business partner and fellow billion-aire Kent Schiffer circled the room with a familiar supermodel, outfitted in matching red tights as Mr. Incredible and Elastagirl. And our local news anchorman was paired with his pretty sidekick, dressed as Woody and Bo Peep from the movie Toy Story.

Many of the guests were dressed as famous characters from superhero movies or nursery rhyme stories, with most of the men playing the more dominant role. *Typical display of macho-entitled privilege*, I thought. *Why does it seem every man who achieves a certain degree of power have to lord it over everyone else, thinking they're better than the rest of us?* My cheeky cowboy costume seemed a perfect counterpoint to the heavy dose of testosterone permeating the room, mocking their oversize male egos as I swung my big dick around like I owned it.

As Hannah and I began mingling with the small cliques scattered around the room, I found it amusing that while most of the women praised my cocky outfit, their male part-ners seemed threatened by it, silently stealing glances at my huge dong while their wives and girlfriends chatted with me comfortably. I wasn't sure if it was because they felt intimi-dated by my outsize genitals, or because they were secretly fantasizing about fucking me.

As more and more people began gravitating toward us, intrigued by my outrageous costume, Hannah slowly drifted off to the other side of the room. I couldn't blame her, with everyone asking me silly questions like what it felt like to be a woman carrying a man's dick. For a while I amused them, swinging my hips from side to side and playfully grabbing my balls, flaunting my male persona.

But I soon tired of the incessant stares and never-ending quips about my tranny disguise, and began looking for an excuse to break away. Just as I was about to excuse myself to go to the ladies' room, the governor and his wife approached our group and introduced themselves. They were dressed in matching his and hers chef outfits, the only difference being that his wife wore a less poofy hat and a backless apron that showed off her sexy ass and legs.

"That's quite a provocative costume," the governor said, extending his hand to me. "I'm Jack Scanlon and this is my wife, Alicia."

"Pleased to meet you, Mr. Governor," I said, quickly seeing through his thin disguise. "But no less daring than your wife's, which I dare say is even *more* revealing."

"In some respects, possibly," he said. "Except you're revealing both sides of the coin."

"Heads *and* tails, you mean?" I smiled.

"In a manner of speaking," he said, temporarily at a loss for words by my sassy attitude. "Are you here alone tonight?"

I scanned the room and noticed Hannah chatting it up with a hunky guest dressed in a Tarzan outfit.

"It seems my partner is out looking for greener pastures. I guess she felt this one had been fully tilled."

"Oh?" the governor said, glancing at my pendulous prick. "Who's been doing most of the figurative plowing—you, or all these other farm animals?"

"At this point, I'd say everybody's just getting the lay of the land," I said, dragging out the metaphor. "Surveying the landscape, deciding the best place to position their hoes."

"I see what you mean," the governor said, his eyes widening from my double entendre. "You seem to be particularly–*ambidextrous* in that respect."

"I'm just having fun pretending what it might be like to cultivate both sides of the field," I said, running my eyes up and down his wife's sexy body before locking eyes with her. "You never know when a particularly fertile plot might need tending."

"Well put, my lady."

"Please—call me Jade," I said, turning my attention to his wife, who'd been staring at my outfit the entire time. "What about you, Alicia? Have you been enjoying the evening so far?"

"Yes," she said, happy to deflect attention away from her overbearing husband for a moment. "So many interesting people and costumes."

"I find yours very alluring also," I said, staring at her plump breasts pressing against the front of her skimpy apron. "But it seems that all your fun parts are hidden from view, at least while we're talking face-to-face. It's only when you turn around that you reveal your adventurous side."

"I guess you'll just have to catch me when my back is turned then," she said, winking at me sexily.

"I'll definitely be keeping a lookout. Hopefully we can catch up later."

As much as I wanted to continue our playful flirtation, I knew I'd never have a chance for some alone time with her as long as I continued to engage them as a couple. Besides, I was getting tired of her husband's thinly veiled sexist comments.

"Will you excuse me for a moment while I use the restroom?"

"Of course," she said. "But be careful in there. It's not as simple for us ladies to pee standing up as it is for the men."

"Not to worry," I smiled. "Fortunately, this thing is easily removed. Though it might be kind of fun to try it just once."

"Will you be using the men's or the ladies' room?" the governor smirked.

"I'm pretty sure the toilets are unisex in this place," I said, gently admonishing him for another chauvinist remark. "Which will be a refreshing change from the usually cramped ladies' rooms we have to endure in other public places. Enjoy your evening. Perhaps we'll see each other a little later."

"We'll look forward to that," the governor smiled.

As I pulled away from the crowd, I shook my head at the impudent tone of the governor, ignoring his beautiful wife while he shamelessly flirted with me. Little did he know that I was far more impressed with Alicia than by the trappings of his high political office. I felt like I needed to wash myself off after dealing with his sexist attitude and while looking for a place to freshen up, I recognized the familiar red and white uniform of the mayor's wife as she waited outside the closed door of an adjacent anteroom. As I approached her from the side, I admired her shapely legs and full bosom pressing against her tight bodice. Her Little Red Riding Hood costume seemed the perfect outfit to highlight her youthful face and figure.

"You'd think we wouldn't have to wait to use a toilet in this place," I said, sauntering up next to her. "There must be at least twenty washrooms in this mansion."

"No doubt," she laughed. "But even in a place like this, with this many guests, unfortunately we ladies still have to wait to use the lavatory." She glanced down at my faux genitalia and smiled. "It's too bad they don't have his and hers toilets like in most public settings. With that getup, you'd probably get away with slipping into the men's room."

"Maybe," I said. "But I'd still have to pee sitting down. I'm just looking to freshen up anyway. I was hoping for a respite from all the overcharged testosterone out there."

"Tell me about it," she nodded. "I've been dealing with city politics from the other side for almost twenty years now. It's still very much an old-boys network in this business. Women are just treated as chattel, to be trotted out as eye candy whenever there's a public relations opportunity like this."

"That's partly why I wore this outfit," I admitted. "I thought it would be kind of fun to swing my own dick around all these heavy hitters at this posh event."

The washroom door suddenly swung open and a woman wearing a Victorian costume brushed past us, sneering at our haughty outfits.

"Judging by the heft of that thing," she said, "I'd say yours is the biggest one here by a large margin. Do you want to join me while I freshen up inside? It looks like the last thing you need right now is to stand outside alone while everybody wags their tongues at you."

"Thanks," I said. scurrying in behind her as we locked the door, giggling like two schoolgirls. "I'm Jade, by the way," I said stretching out my hand.

"Haley," she said, grasping my hand firmly as she smiled into my eyes.

As we leaned in to the doublewide mirror over the marble vanity to check our lipstick and mascara, I noticed Haley's gaze drifting lower to check out my package.

"You know, if it weren't for the straps holding that apparatus onto your hips, I'd swear that thing was real," she said. "It's so life-like. Even your *testicles* look authentic."

"The whole thing is made out of a special latex engineered to mimic real skin. With all the advances in artificial dolls these days, it's amazing what they can do with sex toys."

"Do you mind if I—*touch* it?" she asked.

"I thought you'd never ask."

As I stepped back from the vanity, Haley turned to face me, reaching her hand down to touch my artificial cock.

"My God," she said, squeezing it firmly. "It even *feels* like a real dick. If only it could get hard, I shudder to think how big it would be angry."

As she reached further down to cup my balls, her face came closer to mine, and we kissed. I pressed my tongue into her mouth and she reached lower still, running her fingers over my moist labia. I purred in pleasure, pressing my crotch harder into her hips. She hiked up her skirt, and I was pleasantly surprised to see that she was completely naked underneath. Recognizing my opportunity to have a little fun, I positioned my hand over my right pistol, gently pumping the trigger. Slowly, my synthetic cock began to fill with air and inflate between her legs.

"What the—" Haley gasped, pulling back to see what was happening. "You've got to be kidding me. You can *animate* that thing?"

"In a manner of speaking," I said. "You want to give it a try?"

"*Hell* yes!" she said. "I'm so horny right now, I could fuck just about anything. But first, let me take a closer look at what I'm working with."

As I smiled at her wickedly, I pumped my trigger harder until my organ rose to a full ten inches of erect flesh. Haley couldn't help herself as she fell to the floor and took my member into her mouth while she proceeded to give me a pretend blowjob. As I watched her stretch her lips around my thick pole, I placed my hands behind her head and imagined fucking her face like a man. Although I was being far gentler than most, it was fun fantasizing being in the man's role for a change, having my way with my muse.

"That's it," I purred. "Suck my big cock, baby. Squeeze my balls while I fuck your pretty face."

Without hesitating, Haley reached underneath me and began rubbing my balls against my raging clit. The sensation was not unlike what I imagined a real man would be feeling as she stimulated my sex organ.

"Fuck, yes," I panted. "That feels good, Haley. I want to fuck you so bad."

Suddenly, she stood up and smiled at me.

"That makes *two* of us. I'm so turned-on, I could pop off any second."

She reached behind her, placing her hands on top of the vanity and lifted herself up onto the counter, hiking her skirt all the way up. I took one look at her glistening pussy and leaned in to kiss her passionately. She reached down and pointed my hard pecker toward her opening and when I pressed it into her, she gasped.

"Oh God, Jade," she groaned. "Your cock feels so good. Fill me up with your big dick. I want to feel your balls slapping against my pussy."

Her dirty talk got me even more worked up, and as I pressed my hips forward, she moaned loudly. As we began to grind our hips together, our tongues danced in each other's mouths. Haley flapped her thighs against me as I plowed in and out of her, grinding my clit against the underside of my rubbery balls. While we grunted and moaned with abandon, anybody who might have been waiting to use the restroom must have surely known what was going on inside. But neither one of us cared, lost in the moment by the rising feeling of ecstasy engulfing our joined bodies.

Suddenly, Haley wrapped her legs around my ass and pulled me even deeper inside her pussy.

"*Damn*, girl," she panted. "You're going to make me come with that big thumper of yours. Fill me up while I come all over your pretty pussy."

"Yes," I groaned. "I'm close too. I'm going to cum with you. God damn, I like fucking you."

"Here it comes," Haley moaned. "Take me over the edge."

I grabbed Haley's hips by both sides and pulled her strongly toward me, grinding my cock and balls as hard as I could against her while ramming my cock in and out of her sloshing pussy. Suddenly, a wave of passion rolled over me as my clit began pulsating against the underside of my faux balls.

"Oh God, Haley," I groaned. "Cum with me baby. Come all over my big dick."

"Yes!" Haley howled. "I can feel you pounding my G-spot. It feels soooo good!"

Suddenly, I felt Haley spraying all over my balls and mound as her pussy clenched down over my phallus while we ground our hips against one another. We moaned inside each other's mouths as we locked lips in a tight and passionate kiss. After what seemed like a full minute of shaking and convulsing in each other's arms, our breathing finally returned to normal, while we kissed with me still inside her.

"*Ahem*," a woman's voice called impatiently from outside the door, from someone waiting to use the facilities.

"I guess we'll have to vacate the premises," Haley smiled. "Though I could make love to you all night long."

"Same here," I said. "Let's clean up and get out of here. Maybe we can find a more private place to continue our fun."

While Haley pulled down her skirt and reapplied her smudged lipstick, I unfastened my appendage and washed it under the tap before reattaching it to my mound. When we finally got ourselves put back together, we opened the door and walked past a long line of stunned onlookers as their eyes widened in shock ogling my still-dripping, semi-hard cock.

4

It didn't take long after Haley and I returned to the main ballroom for her husband to spot us. While we giggled amongst ourselves about the pretentious costumes of all the men in the room masking their tiny peckers, the mayor approached us with an angry scowl on his face.

"Where've you been?" he barked at Haley, his ruddy, pockmarked face making his wolf costume look all the more ridiculous. "I've been looking all over for you. There are a lot of prominent people I wanted to introduce you to."

"Jade and I were just freshening up. No need to get your knickers in a twist, dear."

"*Freshening up*?" he said, darting his eyes back and forth between Haley's face and my tumescent cock. "How long does that take? You must have been gone for at least a half hour!"

"Well, you know how we women are when we hang out in the ladies' room," she replied with a straight face. "There's no telling how long it might take to get ourselves put together in front of the mirror. You *do* want me to look pretty and proper for all your important friends, don't you?"

"I—suppose so," he stammered, distracted by my glistening joystick. He grabbed Haley's hand, trying to drag her away from me. "Come, I want you to meet one of my biggest fundraisers, Kent Schiffer."

As he steered Haley toward a gathering in the center of the room, she looked back at me with an apologetic expression, mouthing the words *later*. Soon after, Hannah came up behind me and cupped one of my bare cheeks with her hand.

"What was *that* all about?" she said. "It looked like the Big Bad Wolf was about to bite off his wife's head."

"He might as well have," I huffed. "The way he was acting as if he owned her. All these upper-class snobs seem interested in is congratulating themselves around their buddies while showing off their arm candy."

"He did seem a little distracted by you," Hannah said, noticing Haley peering in my direction with a flushed face. "And he wasn't the *only* one. What kind of trouble did you get into with his wife? You've got a strange glow about you."

"Nothing much," I lied. "We were just freshening up in the ladies' room, looking for an escape from all the overbearing egos in this place."

Hannah looked at me suspiciously, pinching her eyebrows as she peered at my puffy appendage.

"Well, judging by the flush on your chest and the sweat dripping down your ass, I'd say you were up to a little more than just fixing your makeup. If I didn't know better, I'd swear even your *dick* looks more excited than usual."

"We may have been touching up a bit more than just our *faces*," I admitted. "We started admiring each other's costumes and one thing led to another..."

Hannah reached down and squeezed my tumescent dildo, then her eyes widened as her lips curled up into a knowing smile.

"Is it just my imagination, or does it seem a little *bigger* than when we first came in? You better be careful—you could poke somebody's eye out with that thing."

"That's not the only thing it's good for poking," I grinned.

"No way!" she said, stepping back in mock indignation. "You were *fucking* the mayor's wife in the washroom? Did he have any inkling?"

"I don't think so. But judging by how much noise we were making in there, I imagine it won't take long for word to spread around the room."

"Not to worry–just stick with me, girl," Hannah said, moving closer to protect me from everyone's disapproving glares. "If any of these jokers cause you any trouble, I'll give them a batkick to the groin."

"I doubt that'll be necessary," I sighed, catching Hannah's Tarzan friend stealing glances at me from the open bar on the other side of the room. "Most of the men in here seem reluctant to engage me in any kind of conversation, let alone actually approach me in this getup. I don't know if they're more threatened by my provocative outfit or they're just afraid to admit they're attracted to a pretty girl with a big cock."

I noticed Tarzan moving to the other side of the bar to get a clearer look at me. I found it strange that he seemed so focused on me after Hannah had spent so much time with him earlier. Unlike me, I knew she had a preference for men, and I suspected she was hoping to land a wealthy boyfriend at this event.

"What about you?" I said, shifting my position to deflect

Tarzan's gaze. "What kind of trouble have you been getting up to around all these society types?"

"Not as much as I'd like," Hannah frowned. "I've found a few interesting candidates, but so far everybody's been politely keeping their dicks in their pants."

"Well, you know how it is. With all their extra ornamentation, it might be kind of hard to just whip it out. Most of these guys seem to have gone to great lengths to gussy themselves up with all this embellishment."

"I know what you mean," Hannah said, pulling her tight latex skin down uncomfortably under her crotch. "I guess I didn't give this costume as much forethought as I should have. I'm sweating like a pig under here. I have to dismantle the whole thing just to go pee."

"Not exactly conducive to pulling off a quickie in this place," I chuckled.

"Not as easily as you," she grumbled. "You don't have to remove a single stitch of clothing to get your freak on. All you have to do is find a willing accomplice and insert your magic wand."

With Hannah's back turned away from the bar, I saw Tarzan adjusting his equipment under the counter. His loincloth had begun pouching in front of his penis, and he seemed to be getting more and more aroused watching me.

"What about that hunky Tarzan character I saw you flirting with earlier?" I said, hoping to redirect his attention. "He seems worthy of a little deconstruction."

"It crossed my mind, believe me," Hannah said. "But he seemed more interested in talking about everyone else in the room. Either he's just here for the people watching, or he's gay. I mean, I'm still a *catch*, right? Who can resist a sexy chick in this tight outfit? I was practically throwing myself at him."

Tarzan turned away from me holding his hands in front of his crotch, trying to keep his rising member from making too obvious an appearance. Then he suddenly stood up and exited through a door next to the bar.

"He's probably just trying to keep up appearances," I said. "It's a pretty snooty affair, you have to admit. People would likely get their nose out of joint if they caught a couple getting too carried away in public."

"That's what *powder rooms* are for, right?" Hannah grinned.

"Speaking of, I gotta go pee for real this time. Catch up with you in a bit?"

"Sure," Hannah said. "Just try not to dip your dick anywhere it doesn't belong this time. There's no telling what kind of hullabaloo it might generate if one of these heavy hitters caught you getting it on again with another one of their wives."

"Don't worry," I smiled. "I'll be staying far away from the ladies this time."

As soon as I left Hannah, a flock of men suddenly converged on her, no longer threatened by the presence of her sexy androgynous partner. But I was happy for the distraction, because there was something about this Tarzan hunk I needed to check out. He was the first man I'd met at the ball who'd demonstrated any genuine interest in me, and I wanted to see which persona he was more attracted to.

I meandered through the crowd making small talk with some of the guests then I ordered a cocktail at the bar and slipped quietly out the same door I'd seen Tarzan use. It led to a large wine cellar, darkened and chilled to a frigid fifty degrees. I looked around the room, catching sight of Tarzan huddled between two kegs with his hand moving suspiciously between his legs.

I strolled over in his direction and smiled when I noticed his predicament. His cock was at full mast, flapping up over his flimsy loincloth, high up against his belly. I nodded when I saw how well hung he was, his organ standing a good eight inches in length and at least two inches thick.

"Aren't you a bit underdressed for this place?" I asked.

"I suppose so," he said in a shaky voice. "But I didn't know where else to go." He looked down at his crotch with a sheepish expression, vainly trying to cover up his erection. "It seems I'm having a bit of a wardrobe malfunction."

"Is *that* what you call it?" I said. "Can I offer some help? Provide a little body heat at least? You're shivering in that skimpy outfit."

"Maybe," he hesitated, peering down at my even bigger cock hanging down over my naked belly. "At least you can provide some cover if anyone else comes in here."

As if on cue, the door on the other side of the wine cellar opened, and a uniformed waiter entered the room, walking in our direction. He appeared to be looking for a particular bottle, but when he caught sight of the two of us, he stopped and did a double-take. Without pausing, I stepped closer to Tarzan and flung my arms around him, pretending to make out. It was just the cover he needed, and this was the perfect excuse to get a little closer. The waiter smiled as he nodded toward us, then collected his items and exited the room.

"Thanks," Tarzan said, pulling away awkwardly. "This is beyond embarrassing. I can't seem to make this thing go down and I have nothing to cover up with."

"I can't imagine why you'd *want* to," I said, running my fingers over his hard chest muscles. "With a body like this, you should be showing off as much of it as you can."

He glanced down at my full breasts pressing up against him in my tight leather vest.

"I hadn't counted on getting quite so—*aroused* at this event," he stuttered. "I thought I'd be able to keep it together around all these stiff necks. This has never happened to me before in a public place..."

"Not to worry," I said. "This little accident will stay between us. But if you don't mind my asking, may I ask what's gotten you so worked up? I saw you looking in my direction, and all of a sudden you wanted to hide."

"I'm sorry," he said, his face flushing like a teenager. "I just couldn't help staring at you. I find you incredibly sexy, and with so much of you hanging out for everyone to see, I guess I just had a visceral reaction."

"I understand," I said, darting my eyes over his handsome face, finding myself getting surprisingly turned by his shy demeanor. "But which *part* of me were you most attracted to? I'm hanging out on both sides."

"Both," he said, without hesitation. "You have a sexy body and you're absolutely stunning. But there's something especially alluring about a woman flaunting a man's genitals overtop their naked body. It's very—*ballsy* of you."

"You like *cocky* women, do you?" I said, leaning in towards him as I brushed my thick cock against his tight balls.

"In a manner of speaking," he huffed.

"Did you want to play with it?"

"May I?" he said. "I've never really touched another penis before..."

"You mean besides your *own*?" I kidded. "Is that what you were doing in here? Stroking it trying to make it go down before you went back into the ballroom?"

"I was so turned on, I didn't think there was any other way to get myself back together."

"Maybe I can help you with that," I smiled, reaching

down and grasping his throbbing cock with my left hand. "Is this warming you up a little bit?"

"Yes," he panted, clutching my ass while he rocked his hips toward me, trying to create some much-needed friction against his throbbing hard-on. "But you've got goosebumps too. How can I help warm you up?"

I wasn't sure what he had in mind, but I wasn't interested in him fucking me in the usual manner. I'd long been fascinated seeing gay men play with themselves. I found one of the most erotic things was when they rubbed their erect cocks together. Something about the playful jousting of their erogenous parts always got me turned on.

"Well, we're both equipped with similar equipment," I said, raising an eyebrow. "I've always wondered what it would feel like to rub two cocks together..."

"Oh my God," Tarzan said. "I've fantasized about that too. But you're not exactly *functional* in the way most men are—"

"You might be surprised what this ladyboy is capable of," I grinned. "This little package comes equipped with a few extra features."

As I began stroking his hard-on, I squeezed the trigger of the pistol on my right hip, slowly inflating my rising pecker. Tarzan looked down and widened his eyes, seeing my love muscle inflating to its full ten inches. When it reached its maximum length, I placed it against the underside of his prick and began rocking my hips in tandem with his. Even though he was better endowed than most men, my giant phallus looked like an anaconda slithering up next to his garden snake. As the rubbery veins of my dildo rolled over the sensitive flesh on the tip of his rod, he shuddered and emitted a drop of dew out of his hole.

"Uhnnn," he groaned. "This is incredibly hot. I've always

wondered what this would feel like, but to do it with such a sexy woman is a dream come true."

"You've always wanted to get it on with a *tranny*?" I smirked. "Well now you've got your wish."

I reached down and cupped my hands around both of our cocks and began humping him more vigorously. Tarzan groaned as he placed his hands against my chest, squeezing my breasts over my cowboy vest.

"Open it up," I nodded. "See what it's like to fuck a real ladyboy. I want to feel your hard pecs rubbing against my tits."

He didn't need any more encouragement as he fumbled with my buttons until he freed my boobs from their tight enclosure. When he saw my firm breasts bouncing on my chest, he circled them with his hands and pinched my nipples gently while I continued frotting our cocks together in my hands.

"Fucking hell," he said. "You are so hot. You are truly the woman of my dreams."

"And *man* also?" I smiled.

"Yes," he admitted. "I've long fantasized what it would be like to hold another man's penis in my hands."

"Why don't you take the driver's seat then?" I said, acknowledging his bisexual nature. "Let me admire the scenery for a while."

When I removed my hands, he placed his palms around our joined cocks and squeezed them together firmly. More precum oozed out of the head of his pole, and he moaned as he began to pick up the pace of his rocking motion. Neither one of us seemed interested in kissing, fixated on the appearance of our two big cocks frotting in and out of his hands. As he began to moan more loudly, I slapped my sweaty breasts against his hard chest. I could tell he was getting close to the point of no return, and I was eager to watch him cum with our cocks joined together.

"Yes, baby," I purred. "Let it come. Cum all over my big tits. Let me hear Tarzan's call of the wild."

Suddenly, he arched his back and thrust his dick as hard as he could against my organ, pressing his balls tightly against mine. My clit throbbed as he shot one giant geyser after another between my boobs, cumming all over the underside of his chin and face.

"Fuckkkk!" he growled with each spurt. "I'm cumming all over your cock. *Uhn, uhn, uhn!*"

With each throb and spasm, he grunted like a wild animal until he was fully spent. When he finally recovered his strength, he looked up at me with gratitude.

"Thank you," he said. "I needed that. You were even more magnificent than I imagined."

"Glad I could be of service," I said. "Now you should get yourself back in there. Somewhere out there is your *real* Jane, waiting for you to scoop her up and take her away to your jungle."

"What about you?" he said, looking at me confused.

"I'm still looking for my Jane, too," I smiled.

The whole time neither one of us had so much as touched lips. All either one of us wanted was a quickie in the wine cellar, where we could live out one of our mutual boy-on-boy fantasies. As Tarzan tucked his pecker back under his loincloth and staggered out of the cellar, I smiled.

That's one way to get it on with a man, I thought. I wondered what other fantasies awaited me before the night would be over.

5

———

After Tarzan left the wine cellar, I found a sink nearby and cleaned myself up, removing all the cum that he'd splattered over my dildo and chest. Feeling flushed and sweaty, I decided to catch some fresh air before going back into the main room. A side door from the cellar led onto an expansive terrace overlooking the lake. Standing alone in a corner of the balcony stood the governor's wife Alicia with her back toward me. Her arms rested on the stone railing as she puffed a cigarette, leaning over with her naked ass jutting out behind her backless apron. My pussy fluttered as I admired her shapely figure, feeling the moisture accumulating on my lips tingling in the cool autumn air.

Alicia had one of the most magnificent backsides I'd ever beheld. Her long, slender legs were taut and shapely like a professional dancer's and her ass was as tight and firm as a teenager. The rising moonlight reflecting off Lake Michigan shimmered between the space in her thighs, illuminating the dark pit under her mound. It was almost as if she were daring me to approach her and fuck her from behind.

I surveyed the rest of balcony and seeing that we were alone, I began tiptoeing toward her. It was a calm and cloudless night and the light of the full moon shone brightly over the Bannon estate, revealing the splendor of its manicured gardens. Amidst autumn-speckled trees and perfectly manicured flower beds, lay a geometric hedge maze accented with stone sculptures and a flowing water fountain.

I paused for a moment to breathe in the floral scent of the breeze wafting in from the shore. I couldn't imagine a more romantic setting for a private encounter with my pretty temptress. As I edged closer toward her, I stepped on a small pebble and it went skittering over the stone tiles in Alicia's direction. She cocked her head and turned slightly in my direction, then bent lower on the handrail, taking another puff of her cigarette. Whoever she imagined approaching her from behind only increased the boldness of her seductive pose.

Maybe being the wife of the most powerful figure in the state gave her the confidence to blow off any would-be interlopers. Or maybe she was just bored and looking for an anonymous fling to mix up her dull political life. Whatever the reason, her self-assured nature turned me on even more and as the glistening slit of her pussy came into focus, I felt the wetness from my own sex beginning to run down the insides of my thighs. When I came within a few feet of her, she stood up with her arms extended on the balustrade and blew a stream of smoke high in the air.

"Beautiful night, isn't it?" she said to no one in particular.

"Spectacular," I said. "The view is truly magnificent in this light."

"Mmm," she replied, oblivious to the identity of her midnight paramour. "Were you admiring the landscaping?"

"Among other things," I said, staring at her bald snatch. "Everything is so perfectly balanced and neatly trimmed. It really makes you want to pause and appreciate Mother Nature."

Alicia took a step back with one of her legs, arching her ass higher.

"It would be a shame just to *look* at it," she said, "Nature is meant to be immersed in, don't you think?"

"Absolutely," I said, taking a step closer, brushing my bare breasts against her chilly back. "You never know what you might find until you make contact."

"Like the way a woman's nipples pucker when it's cold?"

"Or when they brush against a soft surface," I replied.

"Or her lover's skin," she said

She pressed her ass further toward me and touched my protruding organ, then gasped and turned her head in my direction, checking it before we made eye contact.

"And sometimes—" she mused, recognizing the familiar shape of my leather chaps. "Nature has a way of *surprising* us with her wonderful diversity."

"Do like surprises?" I teased.

"In the right circumstances."

I reached under the front of her apron and squeezed her breasts, pressing my cock harder between her legs. She reached underneath and began stroking my dildo against her wet cleft.

"I particularly like the way nature has a way of adapting to its surroundings—" I said, beginning to inflate my rubber penis with my pistol trigger. "Like the way it expands and contracts to fill the void in any particular situation."

"Yes," Alicia panted, running her hand up and down my giant shaft. "I'd like you to fill *my* void."

By now, my inflatable penis had reached its maximum length and Alicia was busy rubbing the bulbous head against her inflamed clit.

"Fuck me, Jade," she said, dispensing with any further pretense. "I've been fantasizing about you banging me with your beautiful dick all night long."

"As have I," I panted, angling the tip into her dripping opening. I've dreamt of pounding your beautiful ass from the moment we met."

"*Fuck* yes," she grunted, as I pressed myself inside her. "Pound me with your big cowboy dick. Let me feel your balls slapping up against me while you ride me."

As I began to hump her, I marveled at how enthralled all the guests seemed to be with my transgender persona—both male and female. Everyone seemed to want a piece of my girl-cock, no matter how they could get it. While I watched my drumstick pounding in and out of her hole, I had to admit it was kind of fun assuming the male role for a change. There was something strangely empowering about being connected to a man's cock, watching all these strangers bow to my made-up masculinity. As I grasped the sides of her hips and pulled her toward me, she moaned and gyrated her hips, holding on to the rail for support.

"God damn, girl," she hissed. "You feel so good inside me. I've never had a man fill me up quite this way before. I only wish you could cum inside me. I want to hear you get off with me."

There was something about the sight of my big phallus plowing into her tight little ass that was getting me especially worked up. Even though she wasn't providing direct stimulation to my lady parts, I could have come just watching the incredibly sexy scene that was unfolding before my eyes. But I'd been saving up one more special secret. I pressed a button on the inside of my handle and suddenly my balls began vibrating from a battery-operated motor embedded inside. As I pressed my scrotum against her underside, I was instantly taken to a whole new level of excitement.

"Holy shit!" she squealed. "That's *definitely* something no man has ever done to me. Grind your nuts against me, Jade. Trib me with your big fat balls."

"Fuck, yes," I growled, feeling the rising tide of ecstasy building within me.

I couldn't help smiling, acknowledging the multipurpose capability of my male equipment. Not too long ago I was frotting a man with my big firehose, and now I was tribbing a sexy woman with my vibrating balls. For a brief moment, I felt envious of a man's equipment, but as my pussy began throbbing and dripping over my strap-on apparatus, I became acutely aware of my true gender. I leaned forward and rubbed my tits against Alicia's back, pinching and rolling her nipples between my fingers.

"Can you feel my wetness, Alicia?" I panted. "Can you feel how much you're turning me on?"

She reached under my vibrating balls and inserted two fingers inside me, stroking the front of my G-spot.

"Yes," she grunted. "You feel exquisite. You're going to make me come soon. I want to feel you come with me."

"With every part of my body actively engaged in fucking her, I didn't need any further encouragement. Within seconds, a surge of energy coursed through me, as my pussy began clamping down over Alicia's fingers. At the same time, she hunched over and began shaking wildly as she gripped the railing with all her strength.

"Fuck, Jade!" she hissed. "I'm cumming! Pound my ass with your big dick. God, I'm cumming so hard!"

As the two of us grunted and shook in simultaneous orgasm with my buttocks clenching as I pressed my cock deep into her, I suddenly became conscious of the extra light that was being cast onto the terrace from the open windows of the ballroom. When we finally came down from our powerful climax, she turned around and gently kissed me.

"It seems we have an audience," she smiled, directing her eyes toward the adjacent wall.

I peered in the direction of the ballroom and noticed a giant crowd of onlookers staring out the windows with their eyes and mouths agape.

"Good," I said. "It's about time some of these snobs got a taste of the real world outside their sheltered cocoons. "Maybe this will open their minds about the natural order of things."

With that, I lifted Alicia up onto the stone abutment and spread her legs far apart, pressing my still buzzing cock back inside her.

"If they want a show, let's really give them a show."

6

After Alicia and I came a second time in full view of the crowd, we took a moment to compose ourselves then walked back into the main ballroom as if nothing had happened. Neither one of us seemed to care that virtually everyone was staring at us as they continued gossiping in their little cliques. I didn't even bother to refasten my leather vest or deflate my dildo as my breasts bounced freely on my bare chest in tandem with my turgid hard-on.

The two of us approached the bar and ordered matching margaritas then giggled amongst ourselves about the way everyone was trying not to stare as they talked amongst themselves. In spite of the fact that they pretended to carry on normal conversations, it was obvious that they were still highly aroused by our little tête-a-tête.

"I think Mr. Incredible is regretting his wardrobe choice right about now," Alicia chuckled, motioning toward the billionaire and his supermodel girlfriend.

I stole a glance in their direction and noticed Schiffer had a pronounced erection tenting the front of his tights.

"He's looking more like *Mr. Fantastic* with that cucumber wedged between his legs," I joked.

"And check out our favorite newscaster," she said. "It looks like Woody's popping a little Pinocchio of his own."

I peered at the anchorman and noticed him rearranging the front of his denims as a prominent bulge ran down one side of his pant legs.

"Ha," I chuckled. "I bet he's wishing he wore chaps like me."

I had to admit that I was enjoying the attention of all the powerful people in the room, particularly amongst the men who seemed especially attracted by my naked ladyboy costume.

"I don't know about *Jack* though," she said, furrowing her brow as her husband marched toward us with an angry expression on his face. "I have a feeling that his little willie will be even more shriveled than usual after watching you pound me with your big tool."

The governor stormed up to the bar and grabbed Alicia's hand, trying to ignore the pink pole jutting up from my lap.

"What is it, dear?" Alicia said, feigning surprise at her husband's indignation. "I was just enjoying a quiet drink with my new friend."

"That was hardly *quiet*!" he huffed, dragging her off her barstool. "Come on, it's time for us to go."

"But the party was just getting started," Alicia protested. "I was just starting to get warmed up."

The governor glanced down at my flaring joystick then glared at me.

"It looks like the two of you were getting more than just *warmed up*."

"Oh, come on, Jack," Alicia said, trying to resist his advance. "We were just having a little fun. You said that you wanted me to get more comfortable around your political friends."

"Not *that* way!" he fumed. "You've made a fool out of me and embarrassed me in front of all my colleagues!"

Alicia tried to protest, but the governor pulled her away from the bar and stormed toward the entrance. After collecting their coats from the butler, they soon disappeared out the front door. Alarmed by the commotion, Hannah joined me at the bar and sat on Alicia's stool, taking a sip of her cocktail.

"Jesus, Jade," she said, slapping my dripping dildo. "You sure know how to rock the boat in these genteel affairs."

"That's not the *only* boat I was rocking around here," I said. "Were you watching the show like everybody else?"

"How could I miss it?" Hannah chuckled. "It only took one person to catch you fucking the governor's wife before the entire room joined in the spectacle. Not like they could have *ignored* it, with all the grunting and groaning the two of you were doing."

"I wasn't paying much attention. I was kind of lost in the moment."

"You sure looked like it," Hannah said. "I have to say, It was an incredible turn-on watching you fuck her from behind. I could actually see your buttocks shaking when you came." She glanced down at my swollen cock and shook her head. "How does that work, exactly? I thought you were kind of detached from that thing."

"Not as much as you might imagine," I smiled. "Touch my balls to see for yourself."

Hannah placed her hand over my rubber scrotum and I switched on the vibrator, then her eyes suddenly flung open.

"Holy shit!" she said. "That thing really *is* fully animated. What else can it do? Spurt out fake cum?"

"As much as I wish it could, no. But these two extra tricks seem to be providing all the entertainment I need."

"I'd say so, judging by how loud the two of you were howling out there on the balcony. I fact, I've got a little girly hard-on of my own thinking what that would feel like inside me. I don't suppose we could find our own private alcove for a little fun, could we? I'm so horny right now, this costume is practically glued onto my body."

I glanced around the room and noticed that everybody was staring at us with disapproving expressions.

"Why not?" I said. "After that last escapade, it looks like all bets are off. There's not much to hide any more at this point."

I took Hannah's hand and began heading in the direction of the wine cellar, but Steve Bannon and his wife stepped in front of us, smiling like Cheshire Cats.

"It appears you've been enjoying my party even more than I could have imagined," he smirked, peering at my dripping dildo. "You seem to have gotten a rise out of more than a few of our guests this evening. I'd have to say you win the prize for the most inventive costume."

"I have to admit, it's been far less of a stuffy affair than I imagined." I glanced at Genevieve, noticing the slit in the side of her dress looking even more pronounced than before, revealing her hip bone above her barely concealed pussy. "I've found the conversation very stimulating."

"So it would seem," he said, staring at my tumescent totem. "Would you like to join my wife and me for a little nightcap in our private lounge? We've been admiring you all night long and would love to continue the conversation."

"Hmm," I said, raising an eyebrow toward Hannah. "Do you mind if I bring my friend along? We were just about to explore some private time of our own."

Bannon leered at Hannah's costume then smiled at her.

"I don't see why not," he said. "What do you think dear? Would you like to bring another partner into our little meeting?"

"The more the merrier," she smiled, jumping at the chance to have some more alone time with me. "Besides, now it'll be more evenly balanced. I'm not sure I could manage the two of you all by myself."

"Come then," Bannon said, leading us to a private elevator at the base of his stairs.

As we crossed the ballroom floor, the entire room followed our movement while my protruding penis waggled playfully between my legs. When we got in the elevator and the doors closed behind us, Bannon pressed button number four and smiled at Hannah and me.

"You've already explored many of the rooms in my house," he said. "But I think you'll find the view particularly appealing from the top floor."

I glanced toward Hannah and saw that her pupils were already dilated in excitement. I didn't know if she was more impressed by the fact that Bannon's mansion had four floors and a personal elevator or that she was about to participate in a private orgy with the richest man in the Midwest.

When the lift stopped and the doors opened, we both gasped at the view. The elevator opened to an enormous bedroom with floor-to-ceiling windows providing a panoramic view of Lake Michigan. As impressed as I'd been with the view from his main floor balcony, from this elevation the lake seemed to stretch out in every direction forever. But the view on the *inside* was even more spectacular. Bannon's bedroom was almost as large as most people's houses, with giant expressionist paintings hanging on the walls, a huge wood-burning fireplace next to the bed, and a separate bar beside the sliding glass windows.

"Would you like something to drink?" he said, lifting a crystal decanter off the table. "Perhaps a glass of brandy? I've got a thirty-year-old bottle of Hennessey that I've been meaning to open for a special event."

As much as I admired his impressive collection of personal effects, I was far more attracted to the elaborate trimmings of his beautiful wife.

"That would be lovely," I said, smiling at Genevieve.

Bannon handed each of us a large goblet filled with cognac, then he pressed a remote control device and the large window panes began to separate, bringing in a gust of cool air.

"Would you like to move to the balcony? The view is even more magical at this time of the night."

"Sure," I said, checking with Hannah to make sure she was still feeling comfortable. She simply peered back at me with wide eyes and nodded silently. We stepped out onto the deck and Bannon motioned to a wicker settee encircling a bubbling Jacuzzi.

"It might be a bit warmer next to the hot tub," he said, extending his hand toward the tub. "Please—make your-selves comfortable."

Hannan and I took a spot next to one another, while Bannon and his wife sat kitty-corner to us, a few feet to our left. The view of the lake was magnificent with the light of the full moon reflecting off the ripples like an evening sunset on a secluded beach. A cool breeze wafted in from the shore, and I pulled my vest over my exposed abdomen.

"Feel free to dip your toes in the water," he said. "Or climb right in if you prefer. It's chillier outside than usual tonight."

"I wouldn't mind getting out of these boots," I said, kicking off my footwear and placing my feet in the churning water.

Then I turned to Hannah and smiled.

"This feels heavenly, Han. Why don't you join me?"

She motioned to her all-in-one ensemble and frowned.

"It's not quite as simple for me as it is for you."

"Don't be concerned about *us*," Bannon grinned. "We're all adults here. Besides, I think we've seen just about everything already tonight. No one's watching this time besides Genevieve and me."

Hannah peered at me for a moment and I nodded. I'd never known her to be shy in these kinds of circumstances and it didn't take long for her to shed her clothes and slide under the bubbling water.

"Mmm," she purred, glancing up at me. "It's lovely. You should come in. These jets are good for massaging more than just your feet."

I looked toward Bannon and his wife and they smiled with a knowing grin.

"You said you wanted to find a private spot to continue your engagement," he said. "Don't let us stop you. We'll just finish our brandies while you two make yourselves comfortable."

He glanced down at my bobbing tool then peered back up at me.

"Is your equipment waterproof?"

"It should be," I said, winking toward Hannah. "Would you like me to keep it on?"

"I think we would," Bannon grinned. "I'd love to see how you use that thing close-up. How about you, dear? Are you interested in watching Jade play with her magic wand again?"

"Absolutely," Genevieve said, staring me directly in the eye. "I'd love to see her make another pretty girl come with her big man-cock."

I pulled off my chaps and vest and squeezed the trigger on my pistol to re-inflate my shaft to its full length then pressed the button on the handle to turn on the vibrator. Bannon and Genevieve squinted at the humming device, and I smiled at them as I slipped under the surface next to Hannah.

She scooted up next to me and lowered her hand under the water, stroking my phallus as she caressed the inside of my thighs. I turned toward her and we embraced in a passionate kiss. I could feel the jets of the Jacuzzi shooting between our breasts as we rubbed our tits together while she lifted her leg, straddling my hips. Within seconds, she lowered herself onto my pole and wrapped her arms around my back. As she began to rock her hips together with mine, I glanced up and made eye contact with Bannon and his wife. I noticed the front of his toga was tenting between his legs and Genevieve's hand was moving up and down as he smiled lasciviously toward us.

"Damn, Jade," Hannah groaned as I embedded my rod deep inside her. "That thing feels amazing. Fuck me with your big cock. Rub your balls on my cunt. I can feel it vibrating."

"Mmm," I sighed, as her tits mashed up against mine in the swirling water. "Squeeze my dick, Hannah. Let's put on a nice show for our hosts."

By now, Bannon had dispensed with any form of modesty, flinging his toga to the side where I could see his throbbing erection standing up between his spread legs. Judging by the size of his wife's hand, he appeared to have a decent-sized hard-on, but nowhere near as large as my own.

Genevieve had apparently gotten just worked up watching Hannah and me fucking under the swirling water, and before long she kicked off her heels and hiked up her dress, sitting down over her husband's cock while she faced us. As I darted my eyes between her husband's prick thrusting in and out of her pussy and her dark eyes, our mouths began to open in mutual pleasure.

It was an incredible turn-on watching Genevieve's sexy body squirming over her husband's cock as she watched the two of us writhing in the churning water. Whether she was more excited getting fucked by her husband while two pretty girls watched them get it on or by the sight of Hannan and me enjoying ourselves underneath the surface, it didn't matter. Before long, all four of us were moaning loudly as we watched each other fuck our partners with abandon.

Hannah was the first to go off, as she started shaking wildly on my hips.

"Oh God, Jade," she groaned. "I'm cumming! Ram it inside me. Let me feel your balls slap up against me. Uhnnnnnn!"

Seeing Hannah having a powerful orgasm on top of me soon put Bannon over the edge as he grunted with his shaft pulsing inside his wife's pussy. Although he was staring at me, I was more interested in watching the expression on Genevieve's face as she returned my gaze with glassy eyes. I could tell that she was close, but needed a little extra stimulation to reach her goal.

As she locked eyes on me, she placed her hand over the front of her mound and began jerking her protruding nub. As her eyes opened progressively wider, I leaned forward and lifted my ass over one of the jets behind me. While the water gushed against my quivering opening, the vibrating balls pressed against my clit, and I felt a surge of pleasure engulfing my body.

"I'm close," I panted, locking eyes with Bannon's wife. "Come for me, Genevieve. Let me watch you come all over my big dick."

Even though she was planted on her husband's cock, we were both thinking the same thing. In that moment of mutual ecstasy, we were both imagining that it was *my* cock embedded in her pussy instead of her husband's.

"Yes, Jade!" she howled. "I'm cumming! I feel you inside me. I want you so bad. Oh *Gawd*..."

While the four of us panted and groaned in simultaneous climax, I glanced at Bannon, noticing him watching me with a wild look in his eye. Locked on me with laser focus, he had a strange, almost animalistic expression. I wasn't sure what he was channeling at that moment, but I could tell it wasn't his wife he was thinking about.

After we all settled down, Genevieve lifted herself off her husband's cock and slid in the water next to Hannah and me. She cuddled up beside me and her hand disappeared under the water, and soon after I felt her caressing my vibrating dildo. As Hannah leaned over to kiss her, Bannon stood up with his penis dripping a string of cum, motioning with his head inside his bed chamber.

"Why don't we all go back inside?" he said. "There'll be more room for us to play and we can watch each other better on the bed. Something tells me there's still a lot of pent-up energy between you girls."

Genevieve stepped up out of the tub first and led me by the hand into the bedroom as Hannah scampered in behind us, shivering. Bannon returned from his washroom and threw each of us a towel. Then he walked over to the bed and sat on the edge, beckoning for the rest of us to join him.

"Come," he said. "Let's share the wealth. There's plenty to go around."

"What did you have in mind?" I said, raising my eyebrows. After the Tarzan episode, I wasn't sure what part of me he was more interested in.

"There's enough parts between us for us to create an interesting *foursome*, don't you think?" he smirked.

As we all lay down on the bed and began exploring each other's bodies, Bannon seemed immediately drawn to my cock. As he sucked on my nipples, he reached down and began stroking my phallus while he masturbated himself with his other hand. While Hannah and Jenny intertwined their legs and began rubbing their pussies together, Bannon lowered himself down my abdomen until his face was directly in front of my giant pole. Suddenly, he stretched his lips around the head and began sucking it while he jerked his hand over his own dripping dick. Within seconds, he began moaning loudly, as he jetted squirts of cum all over his stomach.

Seeing her husband getting off so quickly again, Genevieve sat up and peered at the two of us with a sly smile.

"You seem quite enamored with Jade's cock, dear. I have an idea, if you're game for a little four-way fun. How would you like a *real* cock inside you this time, Hannah?"

Hannah looked at Genevieve then back at her husband, and smiled. There was little doubt that she'd fantasized about being fucked by the hot billionaire for a long time.

"*Definitely*," she said.

"Lie down face up on the bed," Genevieve instructed. "That way we can *both* have access to you. And *Jade*," she purred, with a gleam in her eye. "Why don't you choose whatever outlet looks most enticing to you among the three of us?"

As Genevieve spread her thighs over Hannah's face and lowered her pussy onto her lips, Bannon pulled Hannah's legs apart and straddled her opening with his dripping dick. As I watched them begin to fuck my best friend like she was a piece of meat, something inside me snapped. There was something about the way Bannon thought he could use her any way he wanted that pissed me off.

Just another self-righteous rich asshole, I thought. *This guy needs to be put in his place.*

As I kneeled behind him watching the two of them grinding their bodies against Hannah, Genevieve looked up at me and smiled. She glanced down toward her husband's ass and nodded. It was almost like she was *begging* me to fuck him from behind.

As the sides of my lips slowly curled up in acknowledgement, I brushed my erect dildo over Bannon's cheeks. Instead of flinching, he leaned further forward until I could see his balls waggling above Hannah's pussy. His asshole puckered as he thrust in and out of her, and for the first time in my life, I sensed the attraction of anal sex. There was something incredibly sexy and empowering about fucking a man up the ass. Now I knew why gay men separated into tops and bottoms. Just as with lesbian couples, one had to be the dominant one and one was meant to be the submissive one.

And *this* time, it was *my* turn to be the dominant one. Only in a way I'd never envisioned.

I lifted the tip of my pole, still glistening with Hannah's juices, and pointed it toward Bannon's opening. As I pressed it against his pucker, he grunted and pushed back gently.

So he likes being fucked by a woman? I thought. *It's time to show him who's really in charge here.*

I grabbed the sides of his hips and slowly pressed my cock deeper inside him. It felt strange and titillating at the same time to be fucking a man with my faux hard-on. As my balls pressed back against my clit, I imagined what it would feel like for a man to fuck another man this way. Suddenly, all the times I'd felt used by men who fucked from behind came flooding back. I thrust my dick as far into Bannon's ass as I could and began pounding my hips against his butt cheeks.

As his hole stretched as far as it could go by my coke-can-width hard-on, I found myself enjoying the feeling of thrusting in and out of him. Strangely, Genevieve seemed to be enjoying the show almost as much as me, as she writhed and moaned on Hannah's face while watching the two of us.

"Yes, Jade," she grunted. "Fuck Jack's ass. Make him your bitch. I want to watch him get off while you have your way with him."

Whether it was the sight of her pretty body twisting over Hannah's face or the sense of power I felt fucking her husband, I soon felt the familiar wall of pleasure beginning to overtake me. As I pressed my balls tight against his ass, creating more friction against my clit, I began to moan approaching my peak.

"Damn this is hot," I grunted. "I'm going to come soon. Watch me cum inside your husband's ass, Genevieve."

"Yes," she groaned, suddenly shifting her gaze to her husband's eyes.

I wasn't sure if she was communing with him at that moment or she just enjoyed seeing him at his most vulnerable moment. Either way, the sight of her convulsing over Hannah's mouth as she reached her own orgasm soon opened my floodgates. I pulled Bannon's ass hard toward me as I thrust my cock one last time deep into him, squirting all over my vibrating balls and Hannah's pussy. Within seconds, all four of us were howling in mutual ecstasy as we pounded and quivered atop one another in a mass of sweaty flesh. When we finally collapsed onto the bed in exhaustion, Genevieve leaned over and kissed me, whispering in my ear.

"Thanks for putting my husband in his rightful place," she mewed. "You have no idea how much both of us needed that."

THE
DARKROOM
AN EROTIC ADVENTURE
VICTORIA RUSH

Everybody's an exhibitionist in disguise...

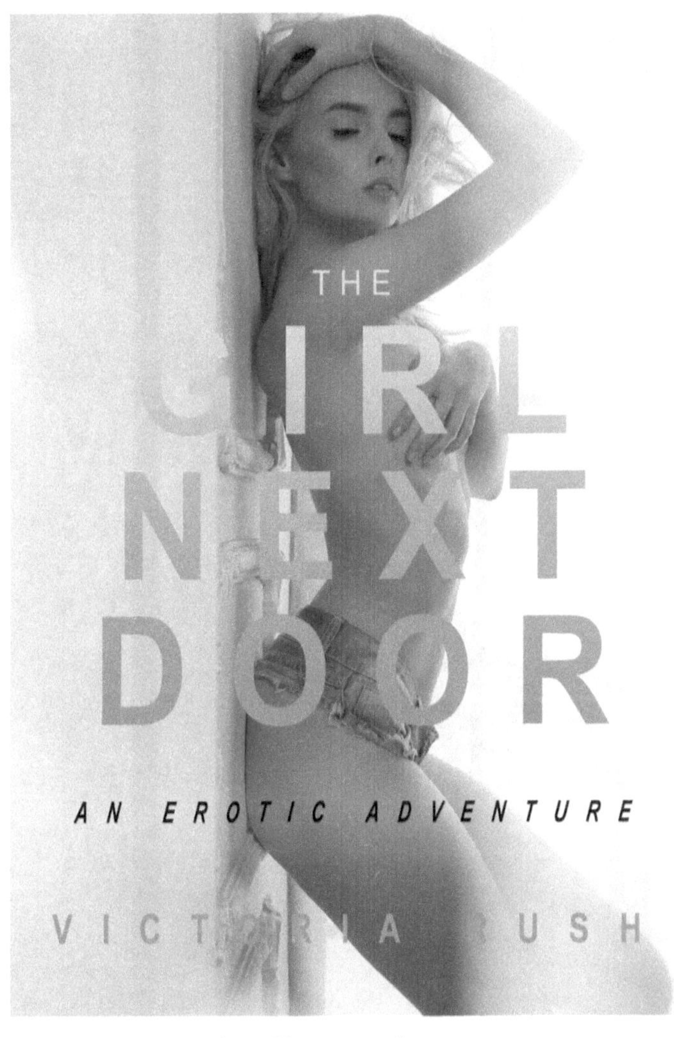

Spying on the neighbors just got a lot more interesting...

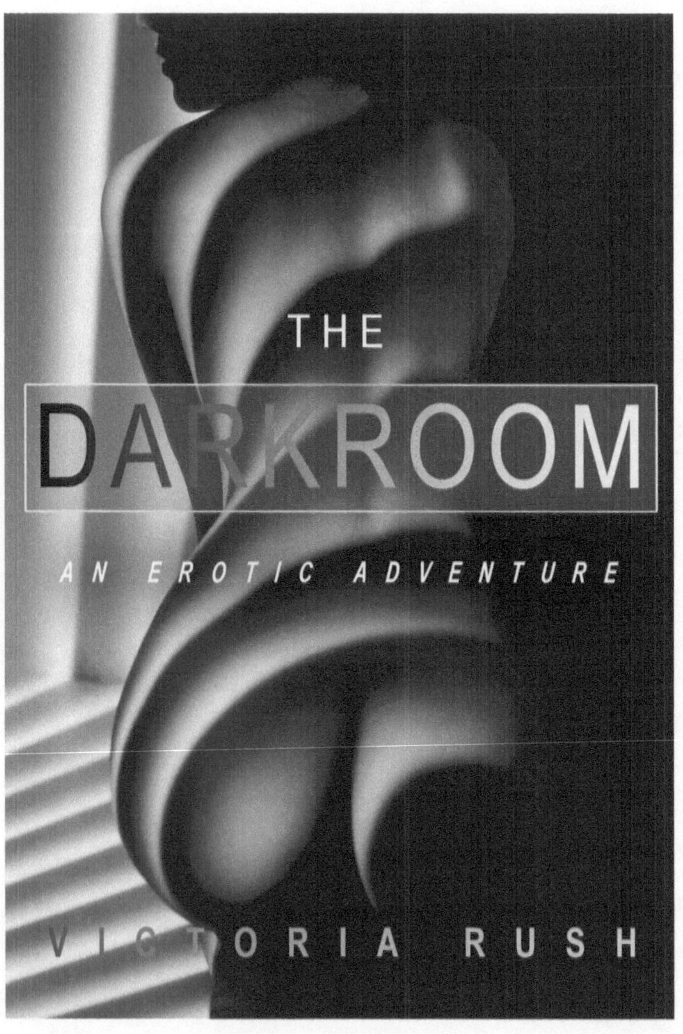

Everything's sexier in the dark...

Artificial intelligence never felt so real...

Books 6 - 10 in the bestselling series - now 60% off.

THE DINNER PARTY - PREVIEW
FINGER FOOD

Sometime later, I heard a soft tap on my bedroom door. Not wanting to remove myself just yet from my cocoon of luxury, I called out to answer.

"Yes?"

"It's time for your massage," a woman's voice replied.

"Just one minute please."

I reluctantly stepped out of the bath and quickly toweled myself dry. I wrapped a large bath sheet around me, re-donned my mask, then opened the bedroom door.

A petite young Asian girl greeted me, wearing a kimono similar to mine and a crimson masquerade mask.

Apparently not everybody who works here always walks around stark naked.

The girl was utterly breathtaking. Long jet-black hair cascaded over high cheekbones past pouty lips, her delicate collarbones peeking from the top of her kimono. I could see her breasts and hips outlined by the tightly-wrapped kimono and suddenly wished that she too had come to my boudoir naked.

"My name is Jasmine," she said. "I'm your personal

masseuse and esthetician. Are you ready for your final preparation?

Just the thought of this beauty laying her tender hands on me sent a shiver down my spine.

"Definitely. Please come in. How would you like me to prepare?"

"Come with me, please."

Jasmine led me into the bathroom, where she nonchalantly removed her kimono and hung it behind the bathroom door.

Oh my God.

I didn't think anyone in this place could get more beautiful or sensuous. Jasmine had perfectly shaped B-cup breasts with a thin indentation running down the center of her perfectly toned stomach. Like everyone else in this place, her pubis was utterly bald and flawless. She barely looked eighteen and I was just about to ask her age, but she spoke first.

"If you'd like to remove your towel and lay face down on the table, we can get started. May I call you Jade?"

There was something about her confident manner and tone that belied her youthful appearance. I had no inhibitions whatsoever about displaying myself unclothed to this stranger.

"Yes, thank you, Jasmine." I unhooked my bath sheet and threw it against the side of the tub.

"Would you like me to drape your backside?" Jasmine asked.

"That won't be necessary," I quickly answered.

Jasmine walked over to the vanity counter and picked up two small bottles of oil resting under an orange radiant lamp. She brought them back to the massage table, opened one, and poured the oil into one cupped hand then rubbed her hands together. The scent of lavender wafted toward my nose.

I closed my eyes in anticipation of her touch. I'd had massages before, but nothing as sensuous and stimulating as this. When her hands touched the small of my back, I jerked reflexively from the sexual tension. My heart was beating a hundred miles an hour as I felt the blood coursing through my veins.

Jasmine must have sensed my nervous tension and began pressing her fingers more firmly into my back as she moved them slowly up each side of my spine. The warm oil allowed her hands to glide effortlessly across my skin. She used every surface of her hands to massage my muscles, expertly kneading my skin with her fingers and palm.

I began to relax as my muscles softened and surrendered to her touch. She sensuously massaged every part of my back, shoulders, and neck, applying just the right amount of pressure. Periodically, she would pour more warm oil on my lower back, dipping her hands in it to replenish the silky lubrication against my pliant skin.

Just as the sexual tension began to subside from the utter relaxation of the massage, Jasmine moved her hands down to my buttocks and began to caress them in soft circular motions. My glutes contracted involuntarily and I unconsciously pressed my mound into the firm padding of the table. Suddenly I was quickly reminded that a gorgeous young woman was caressing my naked body. She cupped each buttock between her hands as she massaged my ass tantalizingly, her little finger sliding slowly into the cleft just above my anus.

Periodically, I'd partially open one of my eyes with my head turned in her direction to look at her gorgeous body. My head was at the same level as her midsection, and my mouth watered as I watched her stomach muscles flex and her hips undulate with each movement of her hands. At times her pussy was almost right beside me and I wanted to reach out and run my own fingers up her soft legs.

I was in total heaven and getting wetter by the moment. Just when I thought I couldn't stand it anymore, she suddenly moved her hands down to my feet and began massaging her thumbs into my soles.

I'd always loved having my feet massaged, but nobody did it like Jasmine. She cradled my foot and used every part of her hands to massage and knead every surface from my heel to my toes. I didn't want her to stop, but there were other parts of my body that were screaming for attention.

As if reading my thoughts, she began moving her hands up toward my calf, using her thumbs to spread the muscle apart. She lingered almost as long on my calf as she had on my foot, rolling the ball of my calf between both of her hands, sliding her slick hands up and down erotically. I couldn't help imagining how she might use those same hands to massage a man's erect cock in a similar manner. My mind wandered again to what pleasures lay in wait for me over dinner.

After shifting her hands to my right leg and giving my other foot and calf similar attention, she placed each hand just behind my knees and began to slowly move them up towards my buttocks. Her thumbs pressed against my inner thighs as she glided tantalizingly close to my apex.

I rolled my legs outward in an invitation to move closer. My legs were parted enough that I was sure she could see my vulva from her vantage point behind me. In my highly aroused state, my lips were engorged and spread apart, revealing my moist and quivering opening.

But as much as I desperately wanted her to, Jasmine

never touched me there. She repeatedly slid her hands right up to the edge of my slit, pressing and rotating her thumbs on the fleshy meat of my upper thighs just below my aching pussy. I suppose this was part of her master plan—to tease me mercilessly and inflame my passions so I'd be ready for just about anything at the main event.

It was certainly working. After thirty minutes of Jasmine's ministrations, I was grinding my pussy into the table trying desperately to give my clit some needed direct stimulation.

Just when I thought I couldn't be teased any more tantalizingly, Jasmine opened one of the bottles of warm oil and poured it directly into the crack of my ass. She paused as the fluid flowed down and directly over my parted lips. I almost came from the gentle movement of the warm liquid as it trickled across the folds of my labia, channeled toward the junction where they joined together at my clit. I shuddered in pleasure at the feeling, even if it was only the subtlest of touch.

Jasmine suddenly interrupted my thoughts.

"Would you like to turn over now?"

It was the first time she had spoken directly to me since the massage started, and it surprised me in my catatonic, pre-orgasmic state. I practically flipped over like a fish out of water and spread my legs expectantly. Finally, I'd get some relief. Surely, she couldn't leave me hanging like this.

"It's time for your final grooming," she said. "I'll need you to part your legs a bit further to provide full access."

Grooming? I knew this was part of the process, but somehow it didn't seem fair to transition at this precise moment. At least I'd be able to stay on the comfortable massage table instead of the clinical vinyl chairs used by my regular esthetician.

Jasmine walked over to another cabinet by the makeup table and withdrew a leather bag from one of the drawers, then brought it back to the table. She reached into the bag and pulled out a cordless hair trimmer.

"Do you have a preference regarding your appearance?" she asked. "Do you prefer natural, neatly trimmed, or bare?"

I knew she was referring to my pubic hair, which I generally kept neatly trimmed. I'd always thought going fully bald was unnatural and unseemly, catering to men's prurient fantasies of fucking young schoolgirls. But in this situation, it seemed entirely appropriate, like I was stripping away all my camouflage and armor.

If tonight was all about being watched, I might as well bare myself in every sense of the word and truly let my inhibitions go. I began to fantasize about rubbing my bare pussy against Jasmine's while she poured warm oil between us. The more work she had to do on me, the more chance I'd have to make this last and hopefully get off.

I didn't hesitate. "Bare, thank you."

"As you wish," she said. "I'll remove the long hairs first with the trimmer, then shave you smooth with a razor."

No waxing? This was different. I was relieved to not have to bear the painful and violent trial of having my hairs ripped out en masse. Although shaving down there was always a scary proposition, I felt safe in the capable and practiced hands of this beautiful esthetician.

Jasmine nodded, then flipped a switch on the trimmer. The device buzzed softly as she placed it gently on my mound. I had only a light dusting of fur and it didn't take long for her to remove it with a few short strokes over my pubis. I shuddered as the vibrations penetrated deep into my core. If she had placed the flat head on my clitoris, I would have popped off in a millisecond. Instead, she turned the trimmer face-down and gently swiped the vibrating teeth against the sides of my vulva, sensuously separating my labia with her hands as she moved the device between my legs to trim the hairs on the inside and outside of my labia.

It was an insanely titillating feeling, but just clinical enough to bring me down from my plateau and shift my focus. My mind wandered to the upcoming feast, and I contemplated what surprises lay in wait at the main event. The hostesses had suggested there would be 'contact' of some sort during the meal, and I was intrigued exactly who and how it would be administered. The idea of being fully bald, cleansed, and thoroughly stimulated going into the event was an incredible rush.

Jasmine continued with the trimmer all the way down my perineum to my anus, barely touching me with the trimmer so as not to pinch any delicate tissues. Apparently there were no parts of my erogenous zone that would remain untouched, now—and perhaps later.

She turned off the trimmer and placed it at the foot of the table. Then she took a bottle of gel from the bag and spread the gel on her hands. Using both hands, she spread it gently between my legs, starting on my mound all the way down to my rosebud.

My body almost levitated above the table as Jasmine finally laid her hands directly on my clitoris. The gel had a mild stinging quality that added to the stimulating sensation. If this was meant to excite my follicles in preparation for the shave, it wasn't the only feature of my anatomy that it made erect. I could feel the hood of my clitoris retract as my button filled with blood and began to push outward. Suddenly, I was fully stimulated again and lusting for Jasmine's touch. I fantasized about her bending down and taking my swollen nub between her puffy lips and letting me come in her mouth.

Unfortunately, my satisfaction would have to wait a little longer. Instead, Jasmine reached into her bag and pulled out a straight-edge razor. In anyone else's hands, it might look threatening, especially in my prostrated and vulnerable position. But something about the way she delicately and sensuously opened the jackknifed tool instantly evaporated my fears. I could see how this type of razor would in fact give her better control safely cutting my stubs instead of the usual ladies plastic razor.

With her right hand, Jasmine gently laid the razor on its flat edge at the top of my mound, while she gently pulled my skin upwards with her other hand. Then she slowly turned the sharp edge perpendicular to my skin and began softly scraping the razor downwards. I could hear the bristling sound as the razor edge removed my nubs right down to the follicles. She repeated the pattern in one inch wide swipes on one side then the other of my pubis, being ever-so-careful to stop just where my clitoris lay quivering in a mixture of fear and excitement. There was something about the utter vulnerability of the procedure that made it the most erotic experience I'd ever had.

Jasmine used the same deft touch as she moved down my vulva and perineum, scraping the vestiges of stray hairs away with gentle swipes of the long blade, while sensuously separating my folds and flesh with her other hand. She took extra time and care around my anus and clit, using the gentlest and slowest motion I've ever felt someone apply to my body. The combination of fright and titillation as she probed my most sensitive body parts created a river of sensuous fluids running down my vulva. By this time, no shaving gel was necessary to provide a smooth gliding surface for the knife.

When she was finished, Jasmine retrieved a fresh wash towel from beside the sink and held it under the warm water faucet then twisted the excess water into the basin. She returned to the table and placed it over my splayed legs then gently cleansed the excess moisture and remaining shaving gel with gentle massaging movements of her hands. The warm, moist towel felt exquisite against my newly shaved skin. Jasmine's hands now felt comforting between my legs rather than erotic.

She had taken me on an incredibly sensuous erotic arc, right to the edge of ecstasy and back, to a quiet relaxed place. I exhaled fully and completely for the first time in almost an hour.

Jasmine removed the towel from between my legs and held up a large hand mirror at a forty-five degree angle toward me.

"What do you think?" she asked.

I tilted my head up and studied her masterpiece. Far from the usual red and swollen vulva that I typically experienced after the violent waxing with my regular esthetician, I'd never seen my pussy look so beautiful. Utterly bereft of any hair, my entire perineum from my pubic mound to my anus was totally bald, pink—and gorgeous. I just stared at my beautiful pussy, utterly transfixed by the transformation.

"You have to *feel* it to really appreciate how beautiful you are, Jade," Jasmine purred.

I moved my right hand down, running my fingers along the edges of my pussy. I gasped from a feeling I'd never felt before. It felt smooth as silk: no bumps or blemishes or cuts or bruises. It was almost as if I was feeling somebody else— somebody I'd never felt before. I couldn't stop my left hand joining the other in rubbing and caressing my sensitive organs.

Jasmine lowered the mirror and smiled at me as I felt the moisture begin to accumulate between my legs again.

"It's almost time for your dinner appointment," she said. "Why don't you save the best for last? I think you'll find plenty of ways to satisfy your appetite over the next couple of hours."

She lifted my kimono from the hook at the edge of the bathtub and held it open for me.

"I'll escort you downstairs now if you're ready. All you need to bring is your kimono and slippers—and your mask of course."

I sat up slowly and stepped off the massage table. Turning around, I held my arms out as Jasmine lifted one arm of the silk robe onto me then the other. Then she turned around to face me, wrapped the silk tie around me, and tied a single bow over my belly button. She retrieved my matching silk slippers and knelt down on one knee to gently lift my feet one at a time and place them softly inside. It took every ounce of my power not to grab her head and pull it into my pulsating pussy.

Jasmine stood up gracefully and smiled into my eyes.

"If you'll follow me, I'll escort you now to the fantasy feast."

She didn't bother putting her own robe on. Her tight little ass barely jiggled as she stepped smartly ahead of me. I wasn't sure if I'd have a chance to feel Jasmine's touch again before the evening was over, but for now I was in total bliss ogling her petite, curvaceous figure from behind...

Read More

ABOUT THE AUTHOR

If you would like to receive notification of new book(s) in Jade's Erotic Adventures, follow me at http://bookbub.com/authors/victoria-rush.

If you have a moment, please post a brief review on my Amazon book page at viewbook.at/tcp . Even just a couple of sentences will help other readers find and enjoy this book as much as you hopefully did.

Follow, share, like, and comment at:

www.facebook.com/authorvictoriarush
www.pinterest.com/authorvictoriarush
www.twitter.com/authorvictoriarush
authorvictoriarush@outlook.com

Hope to see you again soon!